For our art buddies...
- Uncle Paul
- Steve Ol' Boy
- 5·0 Tommer
- mad men matts

—Diggy Dan & Diggy Dave

And a special thank you to my sister
Mikaela for her awesome drawings
— Daniel

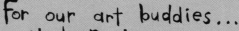

Copyright © 2001 by Daniel Kamish and David Kamish. All rights reserved under International and Pan-American Copyright Conventions. Published in the United States by Random House, Inc., New York, and simultaneously in Canada by Random House of Canada Limited, Toronto.

www.randomhouse.com/kids

Library of Congress Cataloging-in-Publication Data:

Kamish, Daniel.

Diggy Dan / by Daniel and David Kamish

p. cm. — SUMMARY: Dan becomes an archaeologist, a pirate, an Outer Space Man, and other resourceful characters as he clears out the monumental mess in his room.

ISBN 0-375-80576-1 (trade) — ISBN 0-375-90576-6 (lib. bdg.)

[1. Orderliness—Fiction. 2. Cleanliness—Fiction. 3. Imagination—Fiction.] I. Kamish, David. II. Title.

PZ7.K12685 Di 2001 [E]—dc21 00-038710

Printed in the United States of America   March 2001   10 9 8 7 6 5 4 3 2 1

RANDOM HOUSE and colophon are registered trademarks of Random House, Inc.

Diggy Dan

A room-cleaning adventure

by
Daniel and David Kamish

Random House 🏠 New York

Uh-oh! Wrong thing to say. Dan was whisked off to his bedroom, and his door was closed firmly behind him.

Dan admired his messy room. Mountains of toys, clothes, and garbage wobbled as he tiptoed toward his bed.

An unlucky **BUMP** sent the great mounds **CRASHING** to the ground. Toys and clothes covered every inch of the floor. His door and window were sealed shut. It was painfully clear that Dan's only way out was to…

clean his room!

Soooooo…Diggy Dan became an Archaeology Man and started excavating, layer by layer. His digger truck broke open a passage into the Temple of Jumbled Books. Diggy Dan lined up the books, spelling out a code that led to the Tomb of Lost Toys. . . .

"Aye aye, Cap'n. Shipshape it will be,"
said Pirate Dan the Scalawag Man.

"Arrrrgggghhhh!" he bellowed as he tipped over an old bottle of grape soda pop while unrolling his treasure map.

Pirate Dan set sail across the purple sea in a pirate ship pizza....

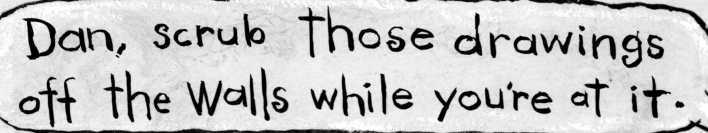

"These aren't just drawings," grunted Caveman Dan the Prehistoric Man. "These are... history," he said as he wiped the wall clean.

Caveman Dan stumbled out into the light of a prehistoric day.
A battle was raging between a Tyrannosaurus fruit snack and
a one-eyed teddy bear. . . .

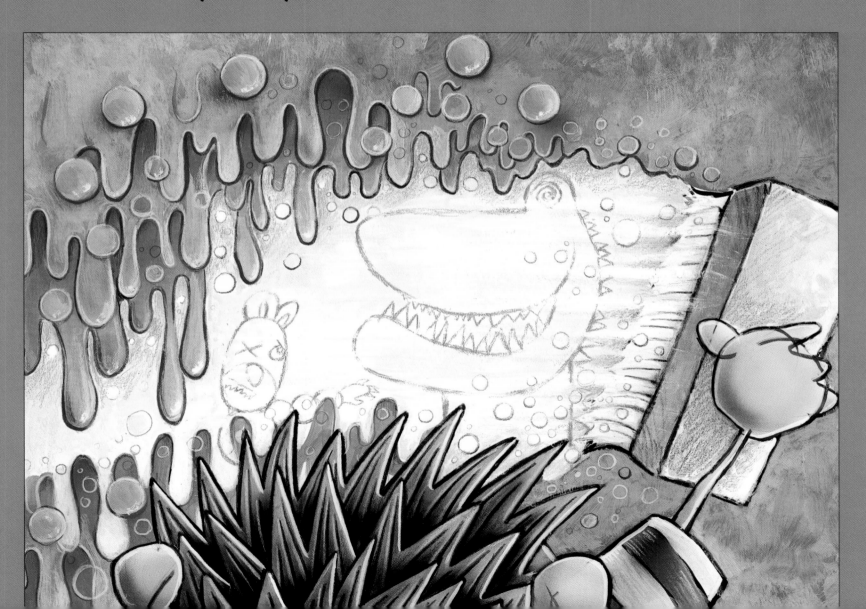

"Affirmative. This space shall be cleaned and secured. Over," responded Rocket Dan the Outer Space Man from aboard his hyper-speed spacecraft.

He **zooMED** out past the Milky Way to a far-off galaxy for a game of soccer against Lord Smiggly's stinky-sock squadron....

Like, dig this crazy jungle jam," sang Swingin' Dan the Rock-'n'-Roll Man.

Spotlights beamed across the stage onto Swingin' Dan and his band. Swingin' Dan jammed on his red bomber guitar as his fans formed a conga line and boogied through the jungle to their seats.

"Why, that would be right friendly of ya,"

drawled Cowboy Dan the Outlaw Man from his dusty Wild West jail cell.

He was in the pokey with two nasty varmints named Rowdy Raccoon and Grimy Gorilla. They told Cowboy Dan how they had been jailed for wearing their underbritches for a week straight and making rude noises at the dinner table.

"White-glove test?" barked General Dan the Four-Star Man. "Four-star generals don't get white-glove tests," he said as he ordered the last toy soldiers into formation and marched them into the closet.

Dan surveyed the room. His bed was made, the floor sparkled, and all the toys, books, and clothes were organized and ready for inspection.

General Dan finally opened his door,
and there was lunch.

After digging into his chow, he
kicked back on his cot.

"This soldier's beat,"

said General Dan as he fought to
keep his eyes open.

"Time for
some R & R...."